MADI MONKEY

LEARNS THE BODY

Written by Dr. Stephanie Liu
Illustrated by Gillian Greenbaum

Madi Monkey Learns the Body
Copyright © 2018 by Stephanie S Liu

Tellwell Talent
www.tellwell.ca

ISBN
978-0-2288-0801-5 (Hardcover)
978-0-2288-0800-8 (Paperback)

To Boo-Boo,
my inspiration.

–Love, Mommy

What are these?

Those are your toes.

What are toes?

Toes help you balance when you walk and run!

What are these?

Those are your knees.

What are knees?

Knees let you bend your legs so you can jump up high!

What are these?

Those are your buttocks.

What are buttocks?

Buttocks cushion you when you have a fall!

What is this?

That is your mouth.

What is a mouth?

A mouth lets you eat, smile, and talk!

What is this?

That is your nose.

What is a nose?

A nose lets you smell to decide what you want to eat!

What are these?

Those are your ears.

What are ears?

Ears let you hear music,
danger, and my voice!

What is all of this?

This is called "Anatomy."

Mommy, I love anatomy!

And I love YOU!